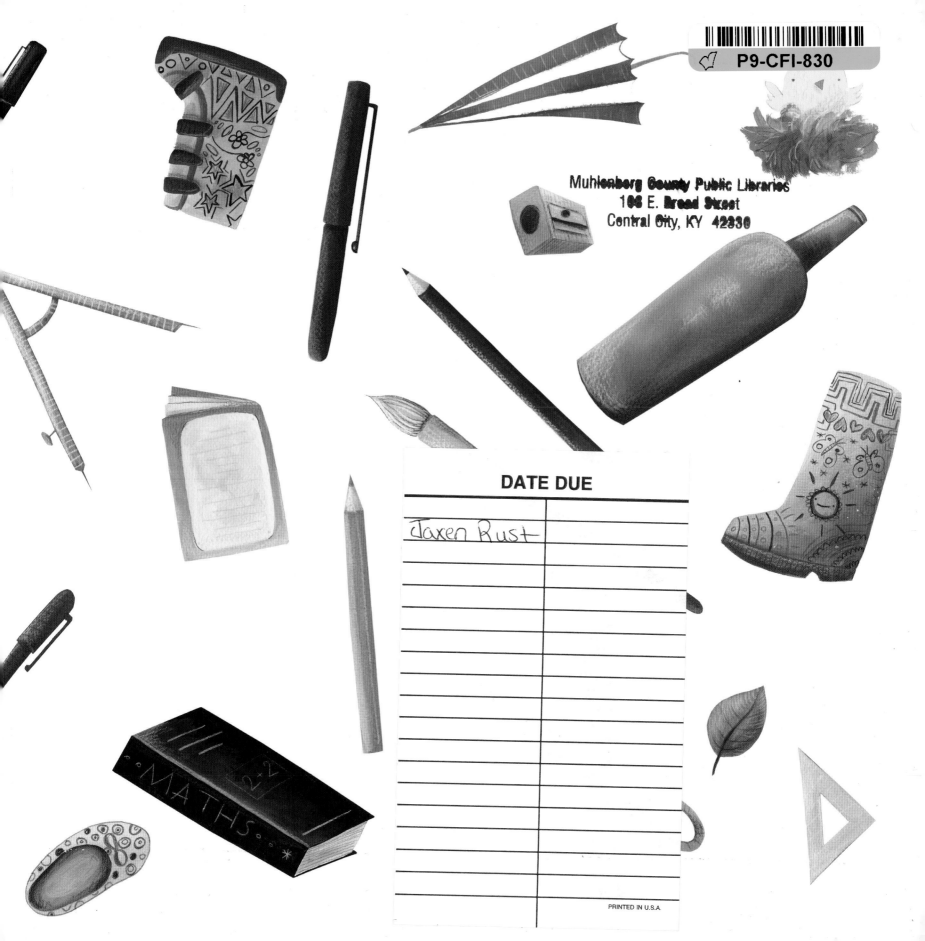

DATE DUE

Jaxen Rust

PRINTED IN U.S.A.

P9-CFI-830

First published in paperback in Great Britain by Digital Leaf in 2012. ISBN: 978-0-9573087-4-9 Text copyright © Anita Pouroulis 2012. Illustrations copyright © Monika Filipina Trzpil 2012. The author and illustrator assert the moral right to be identified as the author and illustrator of the work.

This book belongs to:

_____

digitalleaf
www.digitalleaf.co.uk

PAWS PUBLISHING

For AP who's been through many tangles with me - AP

To my little brother, who is always busy with other things - MFT

Oh, What a Tangle!

Story by
Anita Pouroulis

Illustrated by
Monika Filipina Trzpil

So here we are at the start of our story

About Kiki, a girl with a crowning glory.

Well, that's what her mother had always said;
Kiki thought it had something to do with her head,
Since from there fell hair that was as soft as silk,
Just like a waterfall of chocolate milk.

Mum said to smooth it with a daily brush,
Which Kiki did in the greatest rush
As there was always something better to do,
Like drawing pictures on every right shoe,

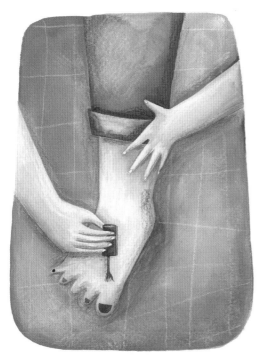

Or painting each toenail a different hue

Or building a toppling tower of pans

Or drawing designs on both of her hands.

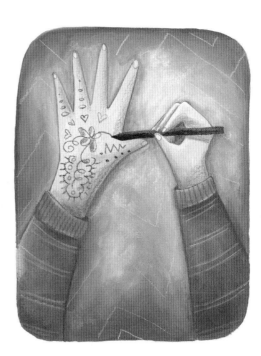

Now, with all of this rushing
Instead of carefully brushing,
Her hair developed a tangled knot,
So small at first it was hard to spot.

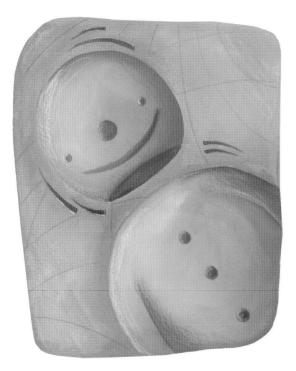

This knot was certainly here to stay,
It was not going to untangle itself away.
And the more Kiki found other things to do,

Like beheading a jelly baby or two,

Or chopping the bristles on her toothbrush

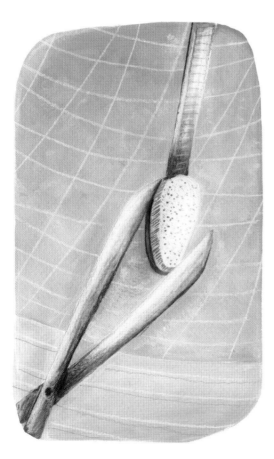

And squeezing toothpaste out in a mush...

...Instead of taking care
Of her beautiful hair,
The bigger and bolder that tangle became
Until poor Kiki didn't look quite the same!

Soon her crowning glory was looking a fright
And doubling up as a pillow at night!
How comfy and convenient,
How cosy and expedient
To have a permanent pillow stuck to her head
So wherever she was, she was ready for bed!

Oh,
what
a
tangle!

As the tangle grew and grew,
Not to mention the artwork on every right shoe,
Kiki found a great way to help her back
For she no longer needed a heavy rucksack!

Now into the tangle went pens and pencils,
Reading books, sharpeners, rulers and stencils!
Oh, how trendy and cool
To be the most unusual girl in school!

Oh, what a tangle!

And another way too that her hair was a boon
She discovered while walking out one afternoon.
When the rain began pouring with all of its might
Kiki learned that her tangle was watertight!

To see raindrops trying to get through that mess
Was actually rather hilarious!
So out into the rain went Kiki to play
(She'd never liked that old raincoat anyway).

Oh, what a tangle!

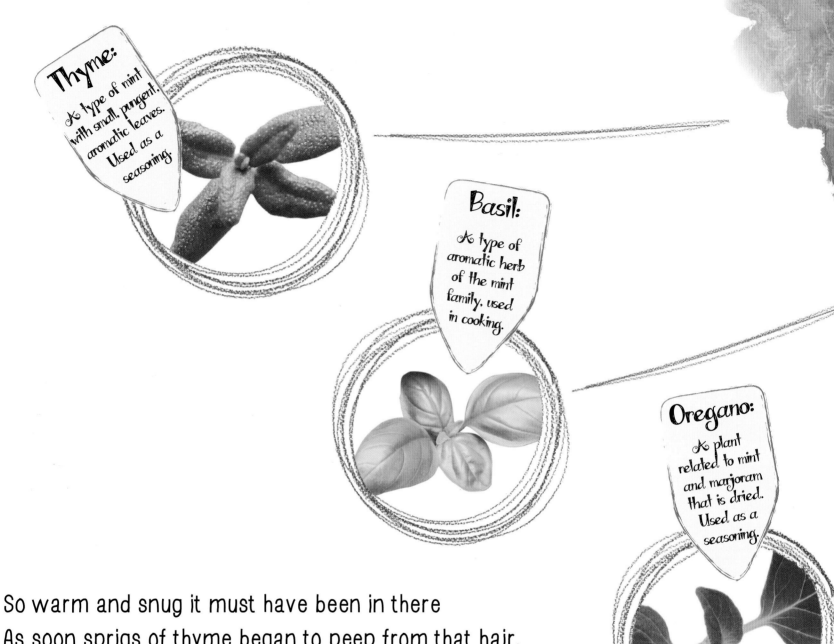

Thyme: A type of mint with small, pungent, aromatic leaves. Used as a seasoning.

Basil: A type of aromatic herb of the mint family, used in cooking.

Oregano: A plant related to mint and marjoram that is dried. Used as a seasoning.

So warm and snug it must have been in there
As soon sprigs of thyme began to peep from that hair,

Not to mention some basil, oregano and mint,
These herbs gave the tangle a slightly green tint!

Soon friends and neighbours were heard to natter
About this very strange and peculiar matter,
"I do beg your pardon...
But you resemble a garden!"

A few days later, little chirps were heard
Then a glimpse of a beak, a feather... a bird!
And not only one, but two, then three
As if Kiki were not a girl, but a tree!

That tangle of hair, that muddle, that mess
Was now doubling up as a bird family's nest!

So Mother Nature was pleased with Kiki's green head
But her OWN mother was really quite angry instead.
"Oh, I can no longer bear to see
That dishevelled mess in front of me!"
How she moaned and filled the air with sighs,
Clicked her tongue and rolled her eyes.

But Kiki, keen to prove her tangle worthwhile
Called to her mum with a great, big smile.
"See Mum how useful my tangle can be,
I can clean those high windows, just wait and see!"

And what happened next was a sight to be seen
As that tangle wiped the windows all clean!
And no one had managed to clean way up there
'Till Kiki walked past with her tangle of hair!

Oh,
what
a
tangle!

But her mother did not smile or clap,
Only looked as if she were about to SNAP!
She said very loudly, "Enough is ENOUGH!
I've just about had it with this huge tangled puff!
How many girls do you know out there
Who like to clean windows with their hair?"

So her mother, distraught and her eyes full of tears
Went in search of her huge gardening shears.
"This tangled mess has got to go,
Why we left it so long, I really don't know!"

And with a snip, the tangle dropped onto the floor,
Giving Kiki a hairstyle she'd not had before.
Yes, her long, tangled hair was there no more.

(See Kiki's other hairstyles on
the interactive app)

So now Kiki's a girl with no crowning glory...
But, oh boy, can she tell an amazing HAIR STORY!

The End

Create your own Kiki hairstyle...

Draw your own hairstyle on Kiki - be as creative and colourful as you like! When you're done scan or photograph your masterpiece and send it to us at funandgames@anitapouroulis.com
The best ones will be posted on our wall of fame www.anitapouroulis.com/tangle

Can you spot the difference?

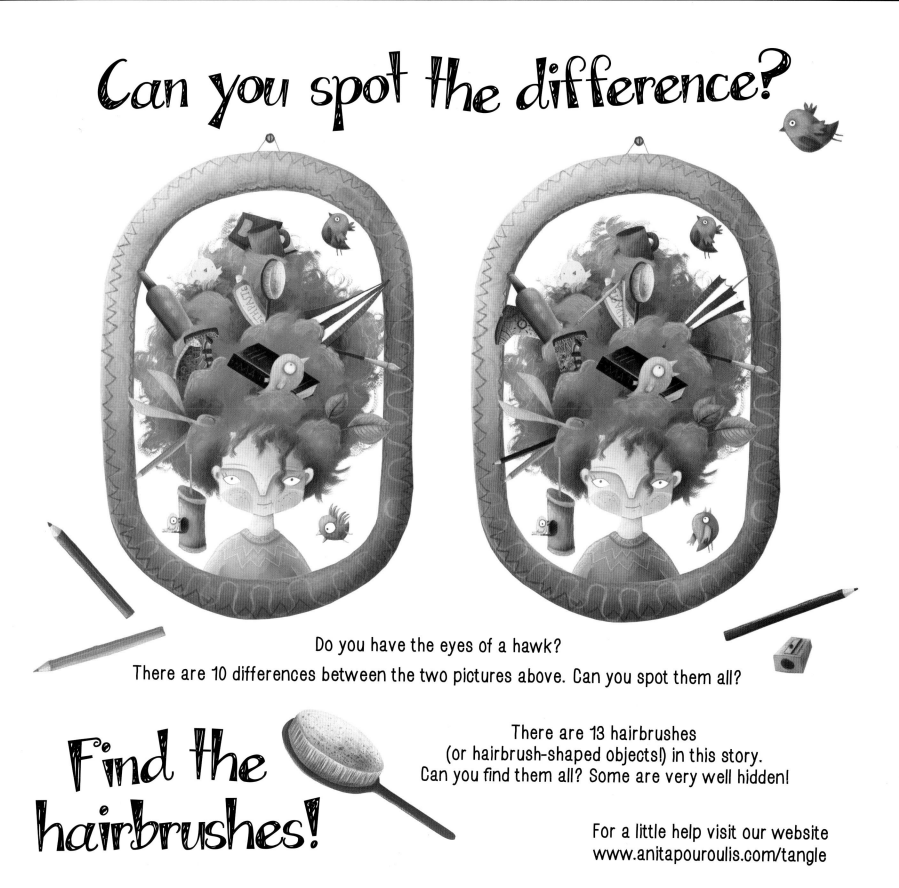

Do you have the eyes of a hawk?
There are 10 differences between the two pictures above. Can you spot them all?

Find the hairbrushes!

There are 13 hairbrushes
(or hairbrush-shaped objects!) in this story.
Can you find them all? Some are very well hidden!

For a little help visit our website
www.anitapouroulis.com/tangle

Oh, What a Tangle! App

If you enjoyed reading this book then check out the interactive app version - available for the ipad, iphone and android devices.

Special Features

- Touch and play - interact with the characters, make them jump into life!
- Narration and word-highlighting option.
- Hear the 'Oh, What a Tangle!' theme music and SFX throughout.
- Find the hairbrushes hidden in the app to unlock the bonus game!

Things To Try

- Play with the bird flying around Kiki's hair.
- Choose Kiki's new hairstyle from a selection of options.
- Drag the items from Kiki's rucksack into her hair!
- Play the bonus game!

Visit www.digitalleaf.co.uk

for more stories and apps

facebook: digitalleafuk twitter: digitalleafuk

digitalleaf
making stories come to life